WHAT YOU POST LASTS FOREVER

Managing Your Social Media Presence

Alexis Burling

Enslow Publishing
101 W. 23rd Street
Suite 240
New York, NY 10011
USA

enslow.com

Published in 2020 by Enslow Publishing, LLC
101 W. 23rd Street, Suite 240, New York, NY 10011

Copyright © 2020 by Enslow Publishing, LLC.

All rights reserved

No part of this book may be reproduced by any means without the written permission of the publisher.

Library of Congress Cataloging-in-Publication Data

Names: Burling, Alexis.
Title: What you post lasts forever: managing your social media presence / Alexis Burling.
Description: New York : Enslow Publishing, 2020. | Series: Social media smarts | Includes bibliographical references and index. | Audience: Grades 5-8.
Identifiers: ISBN 9781978507838 (library bound) | ISBN 9781978507937 (pbk.)
Subjects: LCSH: Social media—Juvenile literature. | Online social networks—Juvenile literature.
Classification: LCC HM742.B88 2020 | DDC 302.23/1—dc23

Printed in the United States of America

To Our Readers: We have done our best to make sure all website addresses in this book were active and appropriate when we went to press. However, the author and the publisher have no control over and assume no liability for the material available on those websites or on any websites they may link to. Any comments or suggestions can be sent by email to customerservice@enslow.com.

Photo Credits: Cover, pp. 1, 40 Rawpixel.com/Shutterstock.com; p. 5 Wachiwit/Shutterstock .com; p. 6 JuliusKiclaitis/Shutterstock.com; p. 9 © iStockphoto.com/oneinchpunch; p. 11 Alexey Boldin/Shutterstock.com; p. 13 Studio concept/Shutterstock.com; p. 16 La1n/Shutterstock.com; p. 18 Jannis Tobias Werner/Shutterstock.com; p. 20 Wolfilser/Shutterstock .com; p. 23 Kevin Dodge/Corbis/Getty Images; p. 25 pixinoo/Shutterstock.com; p. 26 tuthelens/Shutterstock. com; p. 30 fizkes/Shutterstock.com; p. 31 Click Images/Shutterstock .com; p. 35 Ranta Images/ Shutterstock.com; p. 37 Monkey Business Images/Shutterstock.com.

Contents

Introduction 4

Chapter 1
Creating a Digital Footprint. 8

Chapter 2
Is Forever Really. . .Forever? 17

Chapter 3
Smudging Your Digital Footprint 26

Chapter 4
The Future You 34

Chapter Notes 42

Glossary. 44

Further Reading. 46

Index 47

Introduction

In the age of Snapchat, it's tempting to think what you post on social media just … vanishes. You can delete the texts and pics you send to your pals, right? So why can't you erase *everything* whenever the feeling strikes? Unfortunately, most technology doesn't work that way—and neither does social media. Once you post something, it's out there—even if you can't see it.

Take that oh-so-mortifying pic of you at your fifth-grade birthday party. You know, the one with you in all of your rainbow-braces glory making a silly face. While you might purge it from your own Instagram profile, the fact that your pal was the one who posted it—and because it's on other friends' feeds—means the pic is there to stay.

Still not convinced? Say you're fired up about a current political issue and post a YouTube video in which you air your grievances. We'll never bar you from speaking your truth as long as it's respectful. Say it loud; say it proud! But there could be unintended consequences—good *and* bad—if your video goes viral. Once you post content on social media, it's out of your hands. Anyone anywhere in the world can do whatever he or she wants with it, even if it's not to your liking.

Here's the simple truth of it: While the feelings that motivated you to create the video aren't permanent, the mere existence of the post is. Sure, you might think you'll feel a certain way about an issue until you have gray hair down to your knees, but that's not always the case. More importantly, if some stranger

Not everything on social media vanishes like Snapchat's Ghostface Chillah. Most of it is more permanent than you think.

More than 1.9 billion logged-in users worldwide visit YouTube each month. Every day, those people watch more than a billion hours of video. One of those videos could be yours.

or disgruntled person uses the old-you video against the new evolved you, there's not a whole lot you can do about it.

But don't worry. Social media should be fun, not burdensome, and we've got you covered. In this book, you'll learn what a digital footprint is and how it not only reflects your current thoughts and interests, but also how it can shape or impact the person you become in the future. (Hello,

Miss Future CEO!) You'll find tons of helpful tips on what's OK to post, what should totally be avoided, and even a fun quiz. (You're welcome.) We'll also walk you through all the nitty-gritty details about how to tone and hone your digital presence, eradicate posts if you want to clean up your social media history, or even deactivate your profiles altogether if you've just had enough.

Actively managing your social media presence means you're taking full ownership of the way you interact with the world and how the world interacts with you. Say it all together now: Feelings are temporary. But what you post lasts forever.

Creating a Digital Footprint

I f you've done anything at all online—visited your favorite band's website, played a video game, or even read the news—you've created what's called a digital footprint. It sounds ominous, but it's really just a trail of breadcrumbs that shows your internet activity and all the websites you've visited. For adolescents and teens, one of the biggest contributors to their digital footprint is social media.

According to a 2018 Pew Research Center study, 95 percent of teens in the United States own smartphones and 45 percent are online "almost constantly." While 3 percent say they don't use social media at all, about 85 percent use YouTube, 72 percent use Instagram, and 69 percent use Snapchat.[1] Hopping on any one of these apps helps you not only keep up to speed with friends and family, but it also fills you in on what other teens and adults around the world are doing, watching, listening to, thinking about, and buying.

Staying active on social media can have some negative side effects. For example, the number of teens in the United States

Teens are on the web—and social media—All. The. Time. Do you ever long for a screen break or think about the long-term consquences of your posts?

who "often" or "sometimes" encounter racist content on social media has jumped from 43 percent in 2012 to 52 percent in 2018, according to a 2018 study by Common Sense Media.[2] Nearly three-quarters[3] of teens believe tech companies are manipulating content to goad them into spending more time online. More than half[4] of teens admit that apps like Instagram and Twitter are attention hogs because they steal focus away from homework or spending time with friends. And surprisingly enough, only 18 percent[5] of teens say they actually feel better about themselves after using social media.

So why be a part of the social media scene at all? Because it's way fun, almost always informative, and an ever-changing indicator of the latest hottest trends. It's also a great way to express whatever you're thinking or feeling at any given moment—and a chance to get your creative juices flowing when inspiration strikes. #photooftheday

Let's be clear. Social media should never be a free for all. There are rules to follow—and plenty of pitfalls to avoid. Managing your digital footprint sounds easy peasy. But if you want to be responsible about it, it's actually quite the opposite.

Profile Don'ts

To help you understand more about what *not* to do on social media, let's do an experiment. Raise your hand if your favorite thing to read on Facebook is what your friends eat for breakfast every day. How about a play-by-play via Snapchat of your BFF's first date with his crush on Saturday night? Finally, yell "OMG, YES!" if you want a recap on Instagram of your little brother's weekly *Forbidden Island* tournaments with his geek-squad crew, dorky pics included.

Not one hand raised? No spontaneous yells? There's a reason for that. It's because *no one* wants to see those things on social media. Why? One word (well, technically three): #TMI.

Creating a social media profile is super fun. But remember: don't overshare. Not everyone needs to know everything. When you post, be selective.

Don't overpost. Your social media presence shouldn't be a verbal soup of whatever's on your mind at any given second. Instead, it should be well thought out and curated. Just as an artist wouldn't put up her entire portfolio on display (including the elementary doodles) for an art opening, you also don't want to broadcast every single thought or share every little experience you have with the world. We know you're brilliant, but no one's *all that*.

Don't post photos of your friends without first asking their permission. You can ask the same treatment in return. Maybe your BFF wasn't invited to that party you attended on Saturday night and might feel left out. Or maybe you didn't know about the weekend apple-picking jaunt your pals went on. The last thing you want is to unintentionally hurt anyone's feelings—or to have anyone hurt yours.

Don't post photos or videos of yourself naked or doing anything pornographic, suggestive, or in any way demeaning. Okay, this has to be said. Number one, it's illegal. But it's also demoralizing and incriminating. Your body is your temple. Treat it with respect. And remember the internet is for *everyone*. Think about how would you feel if your grandmother, part-time employer, or future college admissions officer saw those photos. Trust us. Do not do it.

Don't post, like, or favorite anything that might be construed as offensive to anyone anywhere, period. That means no jokes, memes, or potentially pointed content about sex, race, color, religion, or gender identity. While you might think it's giggle-worthy, chances are most people outside your social circle will not. Besides, posting that kind of content is not only insensitive, it's cruel. Keep your online humor considerate and respectful at all times.

Profile Do's

We've told you what *not* to do. Next, let's get to the fun stuff and explain what you can do. Do share your intellectual and

Posting a selfie? Consider keeping it positive. Why not show off those pearly whites?

cultural pics and projects. Whether you're outgoing or more on the shy side, social media is an opportunity to express your truest self, if you lean into it. That means letting your brains, your brawn, and your creative sides shine. Your friends and family (and even strangers) might care about the books and articles you're reading, the music you're listening to, or a project you're working on. After all, in this day and age anyone can be an influencer.

Do post selfies if you like them. Just choose those in which you feel your best. Whether it's how you feel inside or how you look outside, exuding self-confidence is key. Create a profile full of pictures of you jamming out at band practice, volunteering on an important project, or spending time with friends and family. But skip the revealing bathing-suit photos. Modesty is always the best route when it comes to projecting your image to the world.

Do retweet or share links with your followers on Twitter or Facebook that reflect what you believe in. What you "like"

Can Your Digital Footprint Affect Your Future? Yes.

Educational testing company Kaplan and CareerBuilder surveyed hundreds of job and college recruiters to find out whether or not they looked at potential candidates' social media profiles before making a decision. The short answer? Yes, definitely. And it is split both ways, 47 percent of college admission officers found info that affected their decision in a positive way. But 42 percent also found info that made them want to say no.[6] The moral here? Be mindful of what you post. Don't put something up that just your friends will think is funny. Imagine everything you post—whether private or not—can be seen by a future employer or your grandma. If it still seems like a good idea, then post away! If you'd shock your gram, time to step away from your phone.

on social media is an integral part of your digital footprint, too. Just make sure your faves don't promote things like hate speech, racism, sexism, or any other form of offensive content.

Take Security Seriously

Now that you have the lowdown on your digital footprint, one of the final (but most important!) guidelines to remember is to keep your privacy and security front and center at all times. You already know to be mindful about your opinions and how others might feel about your posts. It's also crucial that you take precautions to protect yourself online.

Don't post financial or personal information online. Anywhere. No Social Security number. No bank account numbers. Definitely not your home address, school address, or any other address where you can be found. Not only can that info be used against you for physical harm, it could also be stolen by fraud-minded strangers and used for criminal reasons, such as identity theft.

Do set your Instagram, Facebook, and other profiles to either private or friends-only mode. Public profiles can be mined in Google searches and are viewable to anyone who may not have your best interests in mind. Tech reporter Brian X. Chen of the *New York Times* also recommends installing a tracker blocker. "There are add-ons that you can install in your browser that try to block trackers embedded on websites. But be aware that in some cases, they will make parts of websites

When posting anything on social media, privacy should be front and center in your noggin. Check those privacy settings. And it's a good idea to consider using ad and tracker blockers.

work improperly," he writes. "In our tests, Disconnect and Privacy Badger were useful tools for blocking trackers on Google's Chrome browser." [7]

When considering privacy on social media, it's easy to get spooked about what could happen if you're not careful. The golden rule when posting is to take extra precaution whenever possible. If you're still worried, keep in mind these words of wisdom from CEO and founder of BestTechie, Jeff Weisbein: "At the end of the day, everything can be compromised and that's the world we live in now. The best solution is just don't put it online in the first place." [8]

Is Forever Really. . .Forever?

• • •

magine the following scenario: You're a senior in high school and are FREAKING OUT about your college acceptance letters. Which schools will accept you? What if you get rejected by every one and never get a job? But finally the long wait is over. The big day arrives and you check your email. You got the green light from your number one choice! It's time to celebrate.

Then two months later, the unthinkable happens. After looking through your social media profiles, your top pick rescinds its offer. Because of what you and others posted on your supposedly private Facebook feed, you are no longer welcome at that school.

We know what you're thinking. These circumstances sound pretty farfetched. Is some college admissions officer *really* going to take the time to look through every student's digital footprint, especially after the students have already been

College—and other types of further education—can be the ticket to a promising future. Don't muck it up by posting something inappropriate on your social media feed.

accepted? The short answer is: Yes. The situation above actually happened.

In June 2017, Harvard College denied admission to ten previously accepted students based on their social media activity.[1] The prospective members of the Harvard Class of 2021 were part of a secret Facebook group that posted racially, culturally, and sexually insensitive memes. While the group's members insisted the posts were all in good fun and not meant to be serious or an indicator of what members of the group actually believed, Harvard's admission board didn't care. The teens were still given the boot. "Harvard admission is contingent on five conditions enumerated for students upon their acceptance—including one which stipulates admission will be revoked 'if you engage in behavior that brings into question your honesty, maturity, or moral character,'" said Marlyn McGrath Lewis, Harvard's director of undergraduate admissions.[2]

Not all admissions officers at each and every college will scour your social media feeds, especially if said feeds extend back many years. But the lesson here is simple: Don't post anything that could call into question your judgment or moral character. Another *very* important takeaway? What you think is private or erasable might be very far from it. Your online posts have more staying power than you think.

What You Post IS Permanent

Like everything in the world of social media, the permanence of Facebook, Instagram, or YouTube posts is multilayered and sort of unpredictable. On one hand, tweets, videos, and posts can technically be hidden on your profile. In most cases, they can also be deleted from the screen and your profile's history altogether. But just because you remove a post from your own feed doesn't mean it's dead. For one, the metadata still exists

Danger: Off-Limits Posts

Knowing what you can and shouldn't post on social media seems like a breeze. After all, doesn't *everyone* already know that posting racist comments are a bad idea? But it's not just offensive content that should be considered off limits, it's other stuff too.[3] Here are a few other no-no's you might not have thought of:

- Your airline boarding pass
- Your birth certificate
- A confidential email or announcement from work
- Other people's photos or music
- Your creative material that isn't copyrighted

The stamp says it all. On social media, confidentiality should always be a priority.

and in some cases can be resurrected. What is metadata? Basically, it's descriptions of data. It can include info about an image or text that's posted online. This info often helps search engine results, so that you can find what you're looking for. But it can also make something hard to delete.

And don't forget about retweets and shares. If this happens to your post by others before you took it down, it has already taken on a life of its own.

What's more, if a friend takes a screenshot of your post and forwards it to friends or family in a text or email, that content can also be shared again, and again, and again, without your input. "The ready availability of tools to hide teen social media use can be problematic, leading teens to overshare images, videos, and commentary. But that privacy has long been proven to be unreliable," says Ana Homayoun, author of *Social Media Wellness: Helping Teens and Tweens Thrive in an Unbalanced Digital World.* "In the case of the Harvard students, administrators found out about images and messages shared within a private group chat, highlighting how easily information shared behind digital walls can quickly become more public."[4]

Here's another example with different implications. Think about a girl or boy at your school who might have been picked on or shoved inside lockers in elementary school. The bullying might have stopped by the time he or she landed in high school. But the trauma of being harassed and mistreated probably still remains. That same logic applies to online activity.

Words and images have meaning. What you post on social media has far-reaching—and potentially permanent—emotional consequences that can last for years.

Your behavior—whether online or in-person—matters. It shapes who you are now, and who you might become. Therefore, it's important to act responsibly and create a digital footprint that is the best representation of you now and years down the line.

What Others Post Is Permanent, Too

Just as what you post can have a permanent impact, what others post can, too. It's worth repeating that if a pal or family member's posting behavior has you feeling a bit rattled, necessary steps should be taken to mitigate the situation. Have a conversation with them about what's OK to post and what's definitely off limits.

For example, if you don't feel comfortable with your childhood BFF posting a video on your birthday of you doing fake shampoo commercials in your bathrobe when you were six, ask her (nicely) to take it down. Did she get mad? Too bad! *You* have control of you. But remember, if the situation with a post involves a stranger or is more incriminating and potentially criminal, contact the site's administrator and have the image or video blocked and removed immediately.

That slumber shindig at your BFFs was amazing. But do you really want the entire school seeing the post of all of you in your nighties? Maybe not!

Lastly, always pay attention to the app's settings. If you feel antsy about being tagged in others' photos, ask them to refrain from doing so on your behalf. If that doesn't work, most social media apps allow you to either accept or reject a tag once it's been sent your way *before* it appears on your timeline. While that won't solve the problem of your pal's pesky posting habits, it will prevent the pic from showing up on your social media feed.

A Final Word About Data

Finally, a word about data. We know what you're thinking. Asking friends and family not to post is all fine and good. But when something is deleted on social media, where does it go? Is it ever actually ... gone?

Unfortunately, the answer is a little complicated. According to a spokeswoman from Facebook, data can be permanently eradicated. "We make it easy to delete your data—you can delete what you've posted, and we'll remove it from your timeline and from our servers," she said in an interview for *Adweek*. "You can also delete your account at any time."[5]

But other tech experts weighing in on the matter aren't so sure what Facebook is peddling is accurate. There are "backup versions and backups of backups for all social media sites," says Jeff Weisbein. "The way these systems are engineered, it's about redundancy—if one server fails another one picks up where it left off. [Facebook and other sites] might

Account Deactivation & Deletion

How do I deactivate or delete my Facebook account?

Learn More ⟩

While some social media apps state you can delete your account for good, the word is still out on whether the info is actually permanently erased.

have systems in place that go through and delete data, but it might take a long time."[6]

So what to do if you're feeling freaked out by your social media activity or worried it might affect a job interview or college acceptance in the future? In the next chapter, we'll walk you through ways to "smudge" your digital footprint, from taking some chill time away to deactivating your account altogether. You'll also have a chance to take that fun quiz we've been going on about.

Smudging Your Digital Footprint

A re you tired of social media? Have you had enough of "likes" and trying to recruit more followers? Would you rather just have an ice cream cone on a secluded rocky beach somewhere, without your phone and all of its *feedback* for once?

The truth is, you're not alone. While everyone around you might seem like they're nose-glued to their devices, it is not unheard of—nor at all

Sometimes all the likes, tweets, friend requests, and whatnot can get to be TOO MUCH.

lame—to want either a temporary or one-and-done break from it all. Snapchat, Facebook, and all the rest can seem like a real pain in the bum to manage if you're not up for the rat race.

Feeling conflicted about whether to stay or bail? No problem! We've got a solution for every stage of withdrawal. But first, take this quick quiz to help you figure out where you stand.

1. The school dance is a few weeks away and you couldn't be more psyched. In order to prepare, you:
   a. Start a public Facebook group for you and your pals to post pics of everyone looking extra glam in their outfits—the more "likes" the better.
   b. Spend a few days scouring Instagram and various magazines for fashion ideas before going thrift shopping in town.
   c. Go to the mall and buy the first dressy ensemble you see that actually fits.

2. There's a new gal at school whom you have a major crush on but don't know anything about. You:
   a. Immediately try to hit her up on Instagram, Twitter, Snapchat, and Facebook; any girl you like obviously has a profile on all of them.
   b. Ask her friends if she likes anyone and send her a goofy (but adorable) pic on Snapchat; a measured, middle-of-the-road approach has always worked best for you.
   c. Go up to her and introduce yourself in person; face-to-face contact is the most genuine interaction there is.

3. You spend a lot of time thinking about what you want to be when you grow up. When you graduate from college, your dream job would definitely be:
   a. A digital marketing manager for a top fashion designer; influencing and keeping on top of the latest style trends on social media is the absolute best!
   b. A book editor; reading novels and finding new literary talent sounds like the bees' knees; the occasional interaction on social media is fine, if only to be the best you can be at your job.
   c. A primatologist studying silverback gorillas in the jungles of Africa; who needs electricity, let alone social media, when you can spend hours with an ape troop.

4. Your younger brother is coming up in the world and you want to give him some big sibling advice on how to succeed. You tell him:
   a. Pick up as many followers on social media as humanly possible. The more "friends" you have, the better—it's quantity, not quality that matters.
   b. Join a few groups on Instagram or Facebook, but only to meet like-minded people in person. Social media is just a means to an end.
   c. Who needs social media? Going to parties or book readings is a great way to meet new people. Plus, you only need a few gem friends in life—it's quality, not quantity that matters.

5. When you go out to dinner with a friend, your usual approach is:

a. Keep the phone on the table, face up. You never know what you might be missing on Snapchat or Instagram.

b. Keep the phone in your bag and turned on vibrate-only. While you'd rather focus on the present company (and your food!), sometimes it's fun to Google something while you're chatting.

c. Leave your phone at home. The conversation and present company are what's important, not what's happening on your mobile device.

All done with the quiz? Now, tally up your score. Read on to see where you and social media stand in your relationship.

Purge, Baby, Purge

If you answered C for at least three of the four answers above, we hate to say it but we think you've had enough. While many teens check Instagram or Snapchat at least once a day, you want to run as far away from the apps as possible. Why not take the plunge and purge them from your existence?

We've already established that it's not always possible to completely erase your digital footprint. But the good news is that it *is* possible to minimize its impact. If you're sure you and social media are over, there are steps you can take.

The most extreme is to delete your profiles altogether. Facebook, Instagram, and all the other apps have a "delete" option located under Settings. Once you're sure you want to go squeaky clean and close up shop, simply click on the appropriate link and you're good to go.

Had enough of all the chatter? Take a break. The world won't end if you don't check your Facebook account forty-five times a day. We promise!

Some of your photos might still show up in Google searches. Other information, like messages you sent to friends, may also be visible to them after your account has been deleted. Copies of those messages are stored in your friends' or family members' inboxes. But for the most part, your data will be erased—well, supposedly. It still might be stored in some cobwebbed external database somewhere.

Middle of the Road

If you answered B for at least three of the four answers above, it's clear you're on the fence. Some days you want to keep communication lines open. Other days? Not so much. The best approach here is to lean into your wishy-washiness and go middle of the road. That way if you change your mind, you can always jump back in the game with minimal damage done.

There are a few ways to stay engaged while keeping the day-to-day interactions at a low hum. The easiest is to leave everything as is, but change your habits. We know, having the apps on your phone is *way too tempting*, especially if your pals won't go along with your social media detox plan. But once you show some initiative

Feeling kinda Jekyll and Hyde about social media? No worries. It can be a great idea to take a more modersate approach to logging on.

Worried About Privacy?

With all the recent data breaches on Facebook and elsewhere, the world can be a creepy place. If you're worried about privacy protection on social media, but don't want to abstain altogether, there's a few things you can do.[1] First, you can keep your profiles, but change your username. Choose a literary character or other alias by which you wish to be identified. Make sure to alert your friends and family about the change. Second, scrub your timelines of any incriminating information or images you don't want circulated. Third-party apps such as TweetDelete and Social Book Post Manager can help you purge everything you think isn't worth keeping.

and stay adamant about taking a breather, breaking the habit becomes easier by the minute.

If having the apps on your phone is too tempting, delete them to prevent temptation. You can always log on to YouTube or Twitter on your desktop or laptop. Having to make a little bit of extra effort might make a big difference in how much time you actually spend online.

The most extreme of the middle-of-the-road approaches is to deactivate your accounts. In this scenario, all of your posts, pics, videos, and messages stay where they are when you last logged on in case you decide you want to become active again. When the urge to reemerge strikes, all you have to do is sign back in.

Social Media Diva

If you answered A for at least three of the four answers above, our Spidey sense says you're *all about* connecting with others online, so why not embrace it? Attract hordes of new followers. Go hog wild with your digital footprint. Every crowd needs an influencer and chances are, your pals appreciate you for it.

Better yet, you're clearly jazzed about social media. So why not create even more profiles across all platforms? That way you can reflect the many shades and faces of all that is gloriously you? Of course, you need to keep all the safety precautions we already discussed in mind. Keep your profile private. Never post anything inappropriate or too revealing.

But you can have fun on social media. We've got a few examples of social media profiles that you might not have thought of. But don't let our guidelines hem you in. Feel free to experiment.

The Future You

In this day and age, everyone has the potential to be a Renaissance guy or gal. Some people excel at soccer or are into illustrating graphic novels. Others can play piano while singing the alphabet in Swahili. We all have different (and thoroughly fascinating) tastes in food, books, and movies. Whatever your shtick is, the point is that you're most likely a multi-faceted, deeply layered person.

Now that we've established that you're eclectic, here's another mind-blowing concept. Just as you have varied talents and hobbies, you probably also have different personas you project out into the world, right? Would you act the same way around your high school principal as you would your boyfriend? We sure hope not! The same rationale holds true for your social media profiles. One-personality-fits-all certainly doesn't hold true for you in the real world. So why should it be the case on Instagram or elsewhere?

Creating different profiles to reflect your interests—or to replace your personal profile altogether—isn't as tricky as you might think. In fact, the whole shebang can be totally inspiring, entertaining, and yes, easy if you have the right attitude. Sure, it might be a wee bit time-consuming to get all the details and photos together. But once everything is said and done, all you have to do is manage your social media presence—and that's pretty much a no-brainer.

Remember: As with any online undertaking, the same rules apply. Be safe. Be responsible. Always be respectful—and think before you post. Here are a few ideas to get you started.

The Professional You

Do you have dreams of taking over the world someday? Becoming a CEO of a nonprofit organization? Starting your own business? Why not create a profile that reflects your aspirations?

While you probably won't need a LinkedIn profile until at least college, creating a social

Got a strong work ethic? Imagine your profile being super profesh. You could even wear a suit in your profile pic. Dress to impress!

media account strictly for business purposes is a great way to tell the world what you're up to and what you hope to achieve as you move into adulthood. Wear a snazzy, sleek-looking outfit for your profile pic. Add some details about the projects you're working on to your "About" page. If you have any part-time work experience that's relevant to the field you're interested in, throw that in, too. Potential employers love to see a motivated teen strut their stuff.

If you don't have any fieldwork details to post yet, that's totally fine! Populate your feed with articles about business models you find interesting. Don't forget to follow influencers who might be on the lookout for budding entrepreneurs.

The Artsy, Crafty You

If art projects are more your speed, create an online portfolio of your work. You can post images, accompanying text, and even how-to live videos of you working on a particular piece. Whether you're a photographer, painter, potter, or a jewelry maker, there are lots of ways to make your work stand out and look its best.

Into selling your wares? You can do that on social media, too. Facebook has a "Shop" template specifically for legit businesses, complete with an "Events" button that alerts fans to any gallery openings or sales in their area or online. Instagram has a revamped "Shopping" feature where artists and businesses can tag for-sale items in their posts and use "Stories" to show their audience how and where to shop.[1]

Each of these platforms not only exposes you to the work of millions of artists around the world, but they also send these artists your way, too.

"Some social media is aimed at potential clients and can even build direct sales, while others are better at connecting you with the curators and journalists who can give you your next big break. And some are a mix of both, giving you both marketing and networking opportunities," writes Jessica Stewart of *My Modern Met.*[2]

Tools for Managing Social Media Effectively

Whether you're doing it for a business or just to have fun, social media can be overwhelming if you don't know how to manage it. According to Forbes Agency Council, there are four social media management tools, each with paid and free subscription models:[3]

- Hootsuite helps you schedule posts across all platforms.
- Buffer schedules posts to Twitter, Facebook, Instagram, and LinkedIn, and analyzes results.
- TweetDeck assists you in scheduling content on Twitter and helps you follow many conversations at once.
- Google Analytics tracks and reports website traffic and analyzes who's following you.

Love to write? Fill up your profile with your prolific prose. Poetry, short stories, fan fiction. The sky's the limit!

The Writerly You

Is the written word more your jam? One of the best social media platforms for writers is Twitter. Not only can you tweet links to articles or pieces you've written either professionally or on your blog, but you can also follow many reporters, authors, book critics, and publishers. Find a community you jive with. Join in on the literary conversation!

If you haven't published anything, but just want to get in on the game, some publishers even host contests on Facebook, Instagram, and YouTube to give away books. They're always looking for vloggers and social media influencers to get the word out about their authors. Hashtags such as #amreading and #writerscommunity are great for sorting posts related to books, authors, and the general writing process, while #amwriting and #writerslife are better for circulating links to pieces you've written.

The Traveling You

Perusing other people's travel blogs or the vacay pics they post on their Facebook or Instagram feed is perhaps one of the most thrilling activities there is. You can climb Mt. Kilimanjaro in Nepal, feel the romance in the air beneath the Eiffel Tower in Paris, get your peaceful vibes on at Kinkakuji Temple in Kyoto, and even go cliff-diving in Kahekili's Leap in Hawaii—all without leaving the comfort of your armchair. But starting your own travel blog is simple, too. All you need to do is take a trip outside your comfort zone and start recording your thoughts!

  Of course, posting photos of your family's annual summer trip to the lake house in Michigan isn't exactly the most exciting content on social media. But until you get older and can travel on your own, make do with what you have. Highlight what makes the city or town in which you live cool. Write restaurant reviews of where you like to eat. Take a walk around town and post artsy pics or videos of your neighborhood (leaving out any personal details about your street address, of course). Visit a local park and interview the groundskeeper.

Why not have a night out, phone-free? Hang out with your friends and stay logged off the whole time. You might like it!

The sky's the limit! After all, one person's humble backyard is another person's whirlwind vacation.

The Political You

Are you politically active? Do you care about the laws and political movements shaping your community? If so, there are plenty of ways to use social media to engage with other like-minded individuals in your area and beyond.

You can join public or private Facebook groups that are working on issues you're interested in. Or you might read, "like," and retweet articles on Twitter that present carefully researched and well-informed views about something going on in the news. Recruiting people to support a cause is a cinch on social media, too. But no matter what your political agenda might be, make sure the articles you post and the videos you share are based in fact, not hearsay. The last thing you want to be known for is circulating or perpetuating fake news.

And Whatever You Do...

Remember to have fun! However many profiles you create, it's important that you develop a sustainable image you can stand by now and twenty years from now. Identify your audience. Do research about what other blogs or profiles are up to. Most importantly, seek relationships, not just followers. If you're trying to build a brand outside friends and family, optimize your online presence for engagement, not just passive observation. After all, it's called *social* media for a reason.

Chapter Notes

Chapter One: Creating a Digital Footprint

1. Monica Anderson and Jingjing Jiang, "Teens, Social Media & Technology 2018," Pewinternet.org, http://www.pewinternet.org/2018/05/31/teens-social-media-technology-2018/.
2. Rani Molla, "Teens Are Hooked on Social Media. But How Does It Make Them Feel about Themselves?" *Recode*, September 10, 2018, https://www.recode.net/2018/9/10/17826810/social-media-use-teens-time-spent-facebook-instagram-snapchat.
3. Ibid.
4. Ibid.
5. Ibid.
6. Thao Nelson, "Dear Students, What You Post Can Wreck Your Life," *The Conversation*, June 15, 2017, https://theconversation.com/dear-students-what-you-post-can-wreck-your-life-79224.
7. Brian X. Chen, "How to Protect Yourself (and Your Friends) on Facebook," *The New York Times*, March 19, 2018, https://www.nytimes.com/2018/03/19/technology/personaltech/protect-yourself-on-facebook.html.
8. Alissa Fleck, "Your Social Media Data May Be Around for Much Longer Than You Think," *Adweek*, June 26, 2018, https://www.adweek.com/digital/your-social-media-data-may-be-around-for-much-longer-than-you-think/.

Chapter Two: Is Forever Really...Forever?

1. Peter Jacobs, "Harvard Reportedly Rescinded Admissions Offers from At Least 10 students for an Obscene Facebook Chat," *Business Insider*, June 5, 2017, https://www.businessinsider.com/harvard-rescinds-student-acceptances-over-obscene-facebook-memes-2017-6.

2. Ibid.

3. Stephanie Smith, "11 Photos You Should Never, Ever Post on Social Media," *Business Insider*, May 1, 2018, https://www.businessinsider.com/photos-you-should-never-ever-post-on-social-media-2018-5.

4. Ana Homayoun, "The Secret Social Media Lives of Teenagers," *The New York Times*, June 7, 2017, https://www.nytimes.com/2017/06/07/well/family/the-secret-social-media-lives-of-teenagers.html.

5. Alissa Fleck, "Your Social Media Data May Be Around for Much Longer Than You Think," *Adweek*, June 26, 2018, https://www.adweek.com/digital/your-social-media-data-may-be-around-for-much-longer-than-you-think/.

6. Ibid.

Chapter Three: Smudging Your Digital Footprint

1. Brian X. Chen, "Want to Purge Your Social Media Timelines? Can You Spare a Few Hours?," *The New York Times*, March 28, 2018, https://www.nytimes.com/2018/03/28/technology/personaltech/social-media-timeline.html.

Chapter Four: The Future You

1. Rhonda Abrams, "Picture This, Entrepreneurs: Selling Via Instagram," *USA Today*, March 21, 2018, https://www.usatoday.com/story/money/columnist/abrams/2018/03/21/picture-instagram/442265002/.

2. Jessica Stewart, "10 Social Networks You Need to Join If You're a Creative Freelancer," *My Modern Met*, June 1, 2018, https://mymodernmet.com/social-networks-artists/.

3. Forbes Agency Council, "15 Social Media Management Tools That Can Help Your Business Thrive," *Forbes*, May 15, 2017, https://www.forbes.com/sites/forbesagencycouncil/2017/05/15/15-social-media-management-tools-that-can-help-your-business-thrive/#5bbf45312b13.

Glossary

app A software program that is usually used on a smartphone or a tablet computer. (App is short for application.)

curated Selected and presented in an organized fashion.

demoralizing Humiliating.

digital footprint The evidence of a person's online activity.

eradicate Erase completely.

goad Provoke or urge.

hashtags Words or phrases preceded by a hash or pound sign (#) and used on social media sites to identify messages on a specific topic.

identity theft The stealing of a person's private identifying information, usually for financial gain.

influencer Someone on social media who follows and broadcasts the latest trends in order to attract followers.

memes Funny images, videos, or posts that are copied and spread rapidly by internet users.

metadata A set of data that gives information about other data.

mitigate To work out or make less serious.

ominous Threatening; feeling like something bad is going to happen.

pitfalls Hazards or snags; stumbling blocks.

retweet To forward or share a post on Twitter.

selfies Self-portrait photographs.

vloggers People who record themselves talking about their lives and post the content to various video sites, such as YouTube.

Further Reading

Books

Fromm, Megan. *Media Literacy: Privacy and Digital Security.* New York, NY: Rosen Publishing, 2015.

McKee, Jonathan. *The Teen's Guide to Social Media...and Mobile Devices: 21 Tips to Wise Posting in an Insecure World.* Uhrichsville, OH: Shiloh Run Press, 2017.

Nieuwland, Jackson. *Coping with Social Media Anxiety.* New York, NY: Rosen Publishing, 2018.

Websites

Carnegie Cyber Academy
http://www.carnegiecyberacademy.com
An informative website that teaches kids and teens about digital literacy.

Cyberwise
http://www.cyberwise.org/digital-citizenship-games
An info-packed website where kids and teens can play games to learn critical digital citizenship and online life skills.

National Cyber Security Alliance
staysafeonline.org
Provides resources and tips for kids, teens, and adults on how to stay safe online.

Index

A

apps
    as attention hogs, 9–10
    for privacy, 32
    reducing your use of, 29–33
artists, online presence of, 36–37

B

blogs, writing, 38–40
Buffer, 38

C

career profiles, 35–36
college admissions, 14, 17–19
confidentiality, 20

D

data, deleting, 24–25
digital footprints, 8–15, 17–19,
    29–33

F

Facebook, 14–15, 18–21, 24–25,
    27–30, 36–38

G

Google Analytics, 37
Google searches, 15–16, 30

H

Harvard College, 18–19, 21

hashtags, 39
Hootsuite, 37

I

identity theft, 15
influencers, 13, 33, 36, 38–39
Instagram, 8–9, 15, 27–30, 36–39

L

LinkedIn, 35–37

M

memes, inappropriate, 18–19
metadata, 19–21

P

photos
    posting, 12, 14, 20
    tagging, 24
political activism, 40–41
posts
    off-limits topics for, 20
    permanence of, 4–7, 17–25
privacy
    apps for, 32
    of profiles, 15–16
professional profiles, 35–36
profiles
    do's and don'ts for, 10–16
    privacy and, 15–16
    tips for creating, 34–41

publishers, writing for, 38–39

Q
quiz, on social media use, 26–33

R
retweets, 14, 21, 41

S
screenshots, 21
selfies, 14
Snapchat, 4–5, 8, 27, 29
Social Book Post Manager, 32
social media sites
    as attention hogs, 9–10
    colleges' checking of, 14,
       17–19
    creating profiles for, 34–41
    do's and don'ts for, 10–16
    influencers on, 13, 33, 36,
       38–39
    management tools for, 37
    off-limits posts on, 20
    permanence of posts on, 4–7,
       17–25
    quiz for withdrawal from,
       26–33
    statistics on, 8–10

T
tagging, 24
teens
    creating profiles for, 34–41
    statistics on, 8–10
travel blogs, 39–40
TweetDeck, 37
TweetDelete, 32

Twitter, 9, 14, 21, 37–39, 41

W
writing online, 38–39

Y
YouTube, 4–6, 8, 38–39